To my parents, Moses Teel Jr. and Pauline Teel, for their lifelong encouragement and support. Thanks, Daddy, for sharing your story and for allowing me to use it to inspire others. Also, much love to my husband, Joel, for being the "fire" behind my writing, and to my beautiful children, for keeping the flame lit. —P.M.T.

For Kayson Dinkins —E.V.

LEE & LOW BOOKS Inc., 95 Madison Avenue, New York, NY 10016
leeandlow.com

Book design by Christy Hale
Book production by The Kids at Our House
The text is set in Century Old Style
The illustrations are rendered in oil paint on watercolor paper
Manufactured in China by Jade Productions, January 2013
First Edition
10  9  8  7  6  5  4  3  2  1

Library of Congress Cataloging-in-Publication Data
Tuck, Pamela M.
p. cm.
As fast as words could fly / by Pamela M. Tuck ; illustrations by Eric Velasquez. — 1st ed.
Summary: "A fourteen-year-old African American boy in 1960s Greenville, North Carolina, uses his typing skills to make a statement as part of the Civil Rights movement. Based on true events. Includes author's note"—Provided by publisher.
ISBN 978-1-60060-348-8 (hardcover : alk. paper)
[1. Civil rights movements—Fiction. 2. Racism—Fiction. 3. African Americans—Fiction.
4. Typewriting—Fiction. 5. School integration—Fiction. 6. Family life—North Carolina—
Fiction. 7. Greenville (N.C.)—History—20th century—Fiction.] I. Velasquez, Eric, ill.
II. Title.
PZ7.T805As 2013
[Fic]—dc23                              2012030983

JUL 3 0 2013

# As Fast As Words Could Fly

by Pamela M. Tuck

illustrations by
Eric Velasquez

Lee & Low Books Inc.   New York

Trouble was brewing in Greenville, North Carolina. By five o'clock, fourteen-year-old Mason Steele was rushing to finish his schoolwork. Pa would be home from his meeting soon, bringing a new problem. New problems meant more work for Mason. He didn't mind, though, because helping Pa's civil rights group made Mason feel real important.

The screen door banged shut.

"Where's Mason?" Pa asked as he scanned the kitchen.

"Willis, the boy's doing his lessons." Ma sighed.

"I need him to write another letter for me. Ma-s-o-n-n-n!"

"Yes, sir," Mason called. He hurried into the room with paper and a pencil.

"Whittaker's Restaurant refused to serve Matt Duncan's boys,"
Pa explained. "We got to form another sit-in."

Mason took notes while Pa rambled on about what had happened.
Only Mason could make sense out of what Pa said. Later, Mason turned
his notes into a business letter.

"This sounds good enough to send to President Lyndon B. Johnson
himself," Pa boasted after he read Mason's letter.

One evening, after the screen door banged shut, Mason waited for Pa to call him. Instead, he heard Ma and Pa talking quietly.

When Mason finally entered the kitchen, he could hardly believe his eyes.

"A typewriter!" he gasped.

"Yep," Pa said. "The group wanted to give it to you. Said you been quite a little lawyer for us. Figured a typewriter might help you someday."

Mason slid his fingers over the keys. Each row looked like little steps climbing up.

"It's beautiful," Mason whispered. "I'll type the civil rights group a thank-you letter."

"That'll be the right thing to do," Ma agreed.

Soon school was out. During the summer, Mason and his two older brothers, Willis Jr. and Henry, picked tobacco with a few of the white boys who lived nearby. Patrick and Daniel Jones were the only two who acted friendly. They often raced against Mason and his brothers to be the first to fill the mule cart.

In the evenings, Mason was weary from the day's work, but that didn't stop him from practicing his typing. Using his index fingers to pick out the keys, he learned where every letter and symbol was located on the typewriter.

Summer flew by. Before he knew it, Mason started his first year of high school. After the third week, Pa called him and his brothers into the kitchen one evening.

"Boys, I got some real important news for you," he began. "We just won a case we've been fighting for a long time. It ain't right for y'all to be bused twelve miles to Bethel Union High School when Belvoir High ain't but three miles away."

The boys' eyes widened.

"P-P-Pa, you, you know them white folks ain't gonna like us going to their school not one bit," Willis Jr. stammered.

"Like it or not, y'all's going," Pa replied. "Somebody's got to make a change."

The boys stared at one another in disbelief.

"The bus'll be here early Monday morning, so be ready," Pa said as he got up from the table and left the room.

Monday morning, Mason and his brothers were nervous. They watched the school bus come roaring up the road. The driver slowed down just enough for the boys to see the white students on the bus laughing at them. Then he sped up, blowing dust in the boys' faces.

"They just don't want us on their bus," Willis Jr. said.

"I don't want to ride their bus noways," Mason added.

The boys trudged back to the house. When they told Pa the driver hadn't stopped for them, Pa was furious.

The next day, the same thing happened.

The third day, the bus stopped.
Slowly the boys climbed the steps.
"Move it! I ain't got all day," the driver yelled. "And get to the back!"
The boys stumbled over one another as they hustled down the aisle.

Henry spotted a familiar face. "Hey, Patrick," he said.

Patrick didn't answer. He just looked straight ahead.

"You Steele boys are asking for trouble," Daniel whispered.

The driver took off. The sudden motion threw the boys into their seats.

When the boys arrived at Belvoir High, the principal, Mr. Bullock, barricaded the doorway. He looked as if he had smelled a skunk.

"Report to class after the bell rings," he snapped, and thrust their schedules toward them.

"How will we know where to go?" Willis Jr. asked.

"You found a way to get in here, so find your way around." Mr. Bullock turned and stormed into the building.

By the time Mason located the right room, the class had already started. Cold stares and grimaces greeted him when he entered. Mason knew which seat was his: the one in the back corner.

Against the odds, Mason did well in school. He especially liked typing class. The teacher, Mrs. Roberts, ignored him, but he paid strict attention when she helped others. At home, Mason practiced what he had learned. It wasn't long before he needed to earn some money to buy typing paper and other supplies.

Mason found out that the Neighborhood Youth Corps sponsored an after-school program that offered jobs. He applied and received a position in the school library.

"What can you do, boy?" Mrs. Turner, the librarian, asked.

"I can type, ma'am," Mason answered.

"Well, come over here so I can show you what to do."

Mrs. Turner took a stack of index cards and sat down at a typewriter.

"Pay attention, because I'm not going over this with you a second time," she snapped.

Mason had to transfer the information on the spines of books onto the cards. Mrs. Turner typed one card and left him without further instructions.

Two hours later, Mrs. Turner approached Mason. "How's it coming, boy?" she demanded.

Mason handed her his stack of index cards.

Mrs. Turner's eyes bulged. "My goodness! How many cards did you type?"

"I think about one hundred, ma'am," Mason replied.

Mrs. Turner checked the cards. She couldn't find a single mistake.

"Gracious, boy," she said. "You type faster than Mrs. Roberts."

Mrs. Roberts was pleased to be relieved from the library work. She became friendlier to Mason in typing class. She even allowed him to use the new electric typewriter.

The first time Mason used the electric typewriter, the letters jumped onto the paper with the slightest touch. He had to get used to pressing a button to return to the left margin of his paper. He could type faster and more quietly on the electric typewriter, but he missed the tinkling bell on the manual typewriter that signaled a new line.

Mason continued to improve his typing skills. Before long he could type forty words per minute. His job was going well too, and he was earning the money he needed for typing supplies.

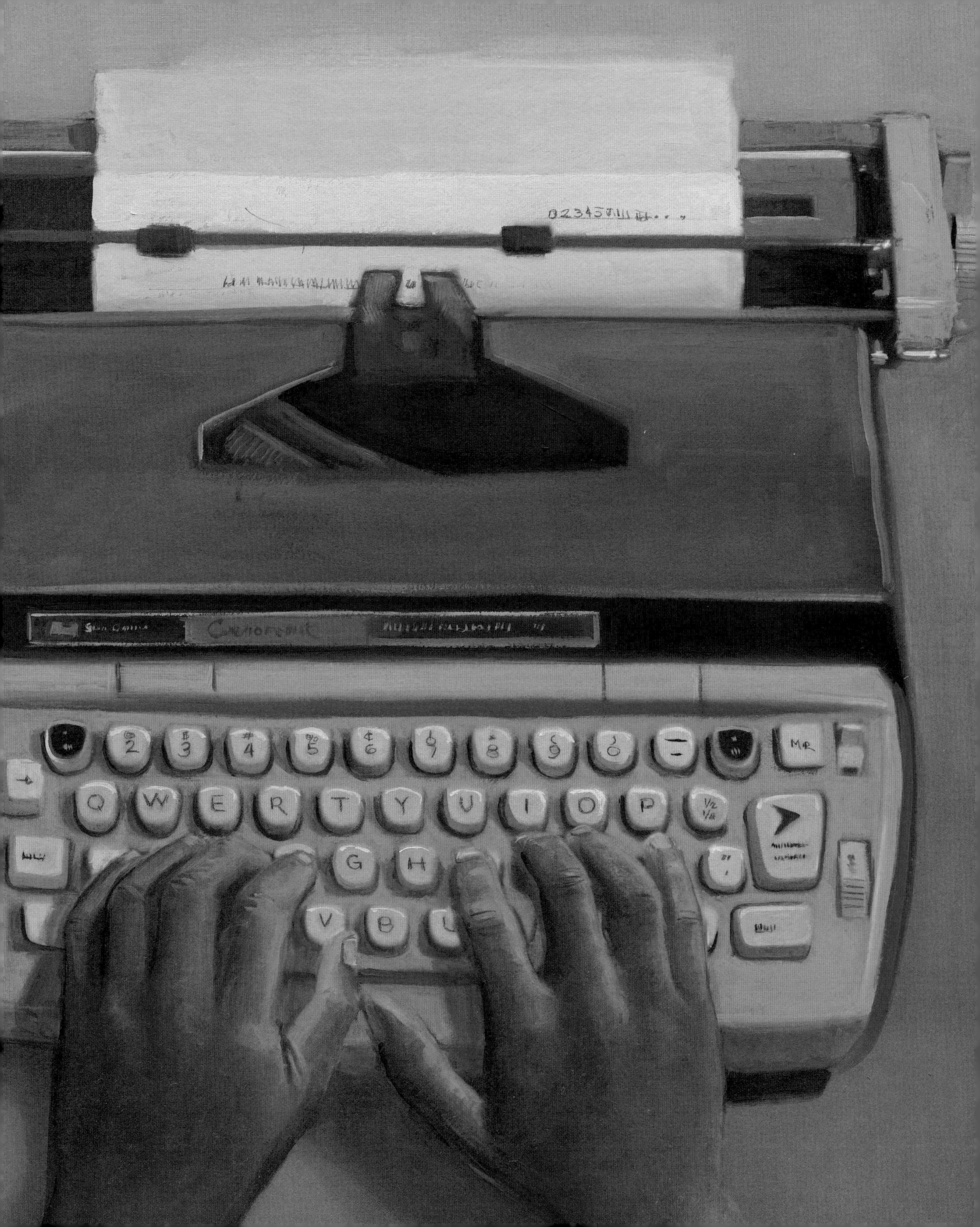
Q W E R T Y U I O P
G H
V B

Then Mason was fired without explanation.

"They done messed with the wrong fella," Pa fumed when he found out what had happened. "I'm gonna call Golden Frinks on this one. He's a field secretary for the SCLC."

Mason had heard plenty of Pa's stories about the Southern Christian Leadership Conference, the organization that coordinated nonviolent action to end segregation. Pa had said that field secretaries interviewed people who complained about unequal treatment. Then they organized a march, a sit-in, or a protest.

"Golden Frinks was personally selected by Dr. Martin Luther King Jr.," Pa added. "And believe me, son, Mr. Frinks shakes ground."

The next morning, Golden Frinks, Pa, and other civil rights workers went to the Board of Education.

An investigation began. The Board of Education discovered that Mrs. Turner's husband didn't want her to stay after school with a Negro boy. The federal government was funding the Youth Corps and now threatened to stop giving the school money for the program because Mason was treated unfairly.

Mason was rehired.

One day in typing class, Mrs. Roberts announced that there was going to be a typing tournament among some of the high schools in the county. The fastest typist in the class would represent Belvoir High.

The students fiercely competed against one another.

Mr. Bullock reviewed the scores. Then he announced the winner. "Mason Steele will represent our school in the typing tournament."

"How can a Negro represent our school?" a student blurted out.

"We can't afford any more trouble with the Board of Education," Mr. Bullock responded, stealing a glance at Mason.

*Do I really want to do this?* Mason thought. But then he recalled Pa's words. *Somebody's got to make a change.*

On the day of the tournament, Mr. Bullock and Mrs. Roberts drove Mason to Farmville High School. Upon entering the auditorium, Mason scanned the room. He tried to ignore the stares of the white students as he considered the selection of electric and manual typewriters.

Mason knew if he chose a manual typewriter, he would lose time. He would have to take his left hand off the keys so he could hit the lever to start each new line. All the other students sat down at electric typewriters. Mason had to make a decision. He closed his eyes to think. His typewriter at home flashed before him.

Mason sat down at a manual typewriter.

The judge went over the rules, then shouted, "Begin!"
*Tap-tap-tap-tap-tap-tap-tap-tap-tap-tap-tap-tap-tap-tap-DING.*
Mason finished his first line. He couldn't hear how fast the other
students were typing. He focused only on his paper.

*Tap-tap-tap-tap-tap-tap-tap-tap-tap-tap-tap-tap-tap-tap-DING.*

*Tap-tap-tap-tap-tap-tap-tap-tap-tap-tap-tap-tap-tap-tap-DING.*

Mason's fingers flew over the keys. His typing echoed throughout the auditorium.

*BZZZZZZZZ!*

"Time's up!" the judge yelled.

All eyes were on Mason as the judge collected the papers.

After a long wait, the results were announced.
"I can't believe this. I really can't believe this,"
the judge said into the microphone. "Mason Steele,

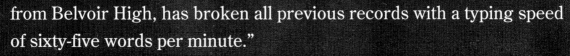

from Belvoir High, has broken all previous records with a typing speed of sixty-five words per minute."

No one cheered. Mason just stared straight ahead.

Mr. Bullock accepted the typing championship plaque for Belvoir High. Not a single person in the audience applauded.

Mason received nothing.

"That's some skill you have, boy," Mrs. Roberts complimented Mason on the drive back to school.

"Thank you, ma'am," Mason responded.

"I just have one question," Mr. Bullock said. "Why in the world did you choose a manual typewriter?"

Mason cleared his throat. "'Cause it reminds me of where I come from, sir."

Neither of the adults said anything more to Mason the rest of the way. But Mason knew his words typed on paper had already spoken for him—loud and clear.

# Author's Note

(A)lthough this story is a work of fiction, it is based on real-life experiences of my father, Moses Teel Jr., during the 1960s.

In 1954, the US Supreme Court ruled in the case of *Brown v. Board of Education* that racial segregation of students in public schools was unconstitutional, and school systems around the country were ordered to desegregate "with all deliberate speed." However, the pace and method of desegregation was left to local and state authorities and district courts. Ten years later, there were still many areas of the country that had seen almost no change. It took passage of the Civil Rights Act of 1964 to strengthen enforcement, along with the federal government's threat to withhold funding to school districts that continued to have separate schools for black and white students. This newfound governmental support enabled substantial progress toward the desegregation of public schools.

In December 1964, my grandfather Moses Teel Sr. filed a lawsuit in the name of one of my father's brothers. The suit, *Teel v. Pitt County (North Carolina) Board of Education*, demanded desegregation of the county's school system. As a result, in June 1965, Pitt County began implementing a court-ordered desegregation plan that allowed parents to choose the schools their children attended. When the new school year began, more than two hundred African American students entered formerly all-white schools. My father and his two brothers were among those students.

My father's fears of attending a formerly all-white school stemmed from a combination of the challenges of high school and the rejection he anticipated. Starting a new school meant more than leaving friends. It meant breaking barriers and making history. Despite the adversity he faced, he worked hard and wasn't afraid to use his typing talent to defy the prejudices of people who considered him inferior. In 1968, my father was one of the first African Americans to graduate from Belvoir-Falkland High School.

The author with her father and a manual typewriter.

Joel Tuck

In my father's day, manual and electric typewriters made writing and office work faster and easier. In the 1980s, personal computers began replacing typewriters for these tasks. Today, computers are used everywhere. Just as technology has advanced over the years, so has my father. He still owns a manual typewriter, but being a man who welcomes change for the better, he has learned to use a computer.

The days of legalized segregation in the United States are over, and our society continues its progress toward tolerance and the acceptance of diversity. My father, and so many other ordinary people like him, played an integral part in moving our country in this direction. Their hard work, determination, and courage set an example for all who face challenges to their rights and freedoms.